W9-AAR-026

The Class with
the Summer Birthdays

Weekly Reader Book Club Presents

DIAN CURTIS REGAN

• • • • • • • • • • • •

THE CLASS WITH THE

SUMMER BIRTHDAYS

ILLUSTRATED BY SUSAN GUEVARA

A Redfeather Book

HENRY HOLT AND COMPANY • NEW YORK

For Linda Allen, with love and thanks — D.C.R.
For Deborah and Megan — S.G.

Special acknowledgment to Officer Rusty Fees,
for the tour of his police car,
and to Keith Salyer,
teacher of the class with the summer birthdays

This book is a presentation of Newfield Publications, Inc.
Newfield Publications offers book clubs for children
from preschool through high school. For further
information write to: **Newfield Publications, Inc.,**
4343 Equity Drive, Columbus, Ohio 43228.

Published by
arrangement with Henry Holt and Company, Inc.
Newfield Publications
is a trademark of Newfield Publications, Inc.
Weekly Reader is a federally registered trademark
of Weekly Reader Corporation.
Printed in the United States of America.

"The Birthday Song" (Bobby Hammack) © 1956 WB Music Corp. (Renewed)
All rights reserved. Used by permission.

Text Copyright © 1991 by Dian Curtis Regan
Illustrations copyright © 1991 by Susan Guevara
All rights reserved, including the right to reproduce
this book or portions thereof in any form.
First edition

Published by Henry Holt and Company, Inc.,
115 West 18th Street, New York, New York 10011.
Published simultaneously in Canada by Fitzhenry & Whiteside Ltd.,
195 Allstate Parkway, Markham, Ontario L3R 4T8.

Library of Congress Cataloging-in-Publication Data
Regan, Dian Curtis.
The class with the summer birthdays / Dian Curtis Regan;
illustrated by Susan Guevara.
(A Redfeather book)
Summary: Because Brittany's third-grade class is made up of
children who were born between May and August, she never gets to
celebrate birthdays during school like other kids do.
ISBN 0-8050-1657-0 (alk. paper)
[1. Birthdays–Fiction. 2. Parties–Fiction. 3. Schools–Fiction.]
I. Guevara, Susan, ill. II. Title. III. Series:
Redfeather books.
PZ7.R25854C1 1991
[Fic]–dc20   90-19670

Henry Holt books are available at special discounts
for bulk purchases for sales promotions, premiums,
fund-raising, or educational use. Special editions
or book excerpts can also be created to specification.

1 3 5 7 9 10 8 6 4 2

Contents

1

Broken Pencils
Equal Bad Luck

Brittany Mackle opened her language arts notebook to the section that said:

Miss McKellips
Grade 3
Seatwork

Snatching a pencil from her desk, she printed her
name at the top of a fresh sheet of paper. As she dotted
the *i* in "Brittany," her pencil lead snapped to the wood
with a dull *pop*.

Brittany hurried to the front of the room to sharpen
her pencil. Turning the handle of the sharpener, she
read the seatwork instructions scrawled across the
chalkboard in Miss McKellips's flowery handwriting:

1. Write three things you like to do.
2. Write three things you don't like to do.
3. Write three things you wonder about.
4. Use complete sentences.

Number four was there because they were learning to write in complete sentences.

She blew on her pencil and returned to her seat.

Staring out a window, Brittany watched a butterfly flutter against the glass while she thought about things she liked. Then she wrote:

> *I like to watch planes take off and land.*
> *I like to ride in Uncle Kevin's police car.*
> *I like all animals, especially reptiles.*

She'd inherited her scaly pets from Uncle Kevin after he moved into a new apartment that didn't allow animals.

Smiling, Brittany remembered the day her class had talked about pets. She was the only one who owned a gecko lizard and a Gila monster. It had made her famous for one whole day.

Next she thought about things she didn't like:

I don't like coconut.
I don't like watching my sister, Shelby, get ready
  for a date.

Glancing around the room, Brittany searched for a clue about something else she didn't like. Her gaze fell upon Miss McKellips's suggestion box on the window ledge. No, she *liked* the idea that any third-grader could make suggestions for their classroom.

Miss McKellips emptied the box on Wednesday afternoons. Then the class voted on that week's suggestions. The teacher always said no to ideas like "Cancel school for the rest of the year."

But a few suggestions had been adopted. Like the one about starting each day with three sharp pencils to cut down on trips to the sharpener. That had been suggested by Sammy Varela.

Brittany continued her search for something she didn't like. She watched Corky Salerno hang the hall pass on the nail by the door and take her seat. Brittany started to write "I don't like Corky," but she knew Miss McKellips would make her change the sentence.

The teacher would also erase one of Brittany's good-citizen marks. When third-graders got ten marks, they could choose from a list of fun things to do.

It was the third week of school, and Brittany had already earned seven. Only one other person had more than seven marks. Teddy Colter.

Cute, funny Teddy Colter. With curly eyelashes and double dimples when he grinned. And his silly way of saying things that made Brittany giggle.

But Teddy was good at doing things behind Miss McKellips's back—like sticking pencils in both his ears while she stacked workbooks in the supply cabinet.

If the teacher saw everything Teddy did, he'd have to pay back all his good-citizen marks—and then some.

Brittany wrote on her paper:

I don't like losing good-citizen marks.

When she dotted the period at the end of her complete sentence, the pencil lead popped again. It reminded her that she'd forgotten to start the day with three sharp pencils.

She searched through her desk, but couldn't find anything else to write with. Clutching the broken pencil, she hurried to the sharpener once more.

"Brittany," Miss McKellips called from the back of

the room. "Didn't you sharpen your pencil a few minutes ago?"

"Yes." Brittany froze, facing the class. Twenty-six
pairs of eyes stared at her.

Teddy snickered. So did Corky.

"Please sit down, then," Miss McKellips said, "and
use a different pencil."

Brittany lowered her head as she walked so the class

wouldn't see her blush. Kids always made a big deal out of it. "Look how red Brittany's face is!" they would tease. Then she'd turn even redder.

Stepping down the aisle, Brittany accidentally bumped into Teddy's desk. His notebook flipped onto the floor.

"Watch where you're going," he hissed.

She slunk to her seat. She hated getting into trouble. Teddy's snippiness only made it worse.

Brittany hooked her thumbnail under the broken wood at the tip of her pencil and peeled it away from the lead on one side. Holding the pencil at a slant, she wrote two things she wondered about:

> *I wonder if I'll stop blushing by the time I get to middle school.*
> *I wonder why Corky doesn't like me anymore.*

She drew squiggles on the corner of her paper and thought some more. Then she wrote:

> *I wonder why I have to be in the class with the summer birthdays.*

2

Friends, Enemies, and Baseball

Brittany checked her paper. All the sentences were complete. She sighed when she read the last line about summer birthdays. Everyone in Miss McKellips's class had been born during the summer months.

That meant they were the babies of the third grade.

Everyone in Ms. Hampton's class had birthdays from September to January, and in Mrs. Beard's class, from February to May.

And they all called Miss McKellips's room the baby class.

But the worst part of all was the birthday parties. It seemed as though the kids in Ms. Hampton's room had birthday parties every week. Their class got to play games and eat treats and sing songs.

Miss McKellips's class got to write in complete sentences.

It wasn't fair.

Brittany turned her paper over and slipped from her desk. She went to the back of the room for a library book to read until the rest of the class finished writing sentences.

Corky was there ahead of her.

Brittany waited while Corky chose a book. Corky's real name was Rachel, but she didn't go by that. She used to have long curls that boinged when you pulled them and let go. But it made her mad when kids pulled on her curls, so she cut her hair short. Real short.

Now kids called her Corky *Boy.* Teddy had started it the first day Corky came to school with short hair, and it made her madder than having her curls boinged.

Of course, Brittany never called her that. The two used to be best friends, until last week, when Sammy Varela asked her if Corky liked Teddy Colter. Brittany had said yes.

It was true. She hadn't known it was a secret. The *real* secret was that Brittany liked Teddy Colter too, but she didn't want Corky to know. Her friend would say she copied.

To make matters worse, Brittany accidentally called Corky "Rachel" in front of everyone on the school bus.

It was hard not to, because Corky's family called her Rachel.

Brittany had spent the night before at the Salernos' house, and heard nothing but *Rachel, Rachel, Rachel* all evening. No wonder she'd slipped the next morning.

Corky had been so angry, she'd hopped off the bus and kicked it. Then she vowed never to speak to Brittany again.

Sighing, Brittany watched Corky choose a book. She liked her ex-best friend's new haircut. But from the back, Corky *did* look like a boy.

Brittany missed sharing jokes and secrets with her. She remembered the last joke Corky told her the night Brittany stayed over: What's a sleeping brontosaurus called? A dinosnore.

She chuckled.

Corky whipped around. "What's so funny?"

"Uh . . . um," Brittany stuttered. She didn't know she'd laughed out loud. "Nothing, I—"

"Whatever you're thinking, I bounce it back double to you." Corky swished past Brittany, almost knocking her over.

Brittany's face grew warm. She turned toward the wall so no one would laugh at her red cheeks.

Double-bouncing back a joke certainly wouldn't harm her. Good thing she wasn't thinking something nasty about Corky.

Biting her lip, Brittany grabbed a book without looking at it and hurried back to her desk.

"Please exchange notebooks with the person next to you," Miss McKellips said.

After three minutes of papers rustling, pencils dropping, and kids whispering, she continued. "Correct your classmate's paper by putting a C next to every complete sentence and a check next to the incomplete sentences."

She demonstrated on the board: C or $\vee$.

Brittany looked at the notebook in front of her. It belonged to Teddy Colter. Teddy Colter was one of the reasons Corky wasn't her friend anymore.

Brittany read Teddy's sentences:

> *I like to play baseball.*
> *I like to watch baseball on television.*
> *I like to go to baseball games.*

She giggled. Teddy was making funny faces at her. Two of his front teeth were missing, which made him look even sillier. She smiled at him and put a C next to each sentence. Then she read on:

> *I don't like rainy days because I can't play baseball.*
> *I don't like November to March because there aren't any baseball games on television.*
> *I don't like days when my mom washes my baseball shirts and I can't wear them.*

She glanced at him. Today he was wearing a Boston Red Sox T-shirt.

She turned to his "I wonder" sentences:

> *I wonder if I'll ever play in the big leagues.*
> *I wonder if I'll turn a double play next summer.*
> *I wonder when the New York Yankees shirt I*
>   *sent away for will come in the mail.*

Brittany wondered if Teddy Colter thought about anything besides baseball. She finished marking Cs on his paper because all his sentences were complete. She hoped he was giving her Cs too.

Suddenly the classroom door burst open. Two ladies rushed in. The first one wore a knee-length T-shirt with the words HAPPY BIRTHDAY! printed all over it in rainbow colors. She carried a tray of cupcakes with pink icing.

The second lady carried a box of funny hats and party favors. A cardboard peacock hat with real purple feathers perched on top of her head.

"We get to have a party!" Cid Quintana yelped as she clapped her hands.

Miss McKellips stared at the ladies, a puzzled look on her face. "May I help you?" she asked.

"Ms. Hampton," the purple-peacock lady said, "I'm

Craig's mother, and this is Lee's mom. We've brought dessert and games for Craig's birthday party."

"Oh!" Miss McKellips exclaimed, herding them back toward the door. "I'm not Ms. Hampton. She's next door. You've got the wrong room."

Groans filled the air as the mothers left.

"We *never* get birthday parties," Sammy Varela hissed in a loud whisper.

Brittany agreed, slumping in her chair. She'd give

up her beloved glass-horse collection if only their room could have parties like other classes.

Groans turned into chattering. Everyone had plenty of complaints about being in the baby class.

Miss McKellips didn't say anything. She picked up an eraser and moved toward the good-citizen chart. The chattering shut off like a light switch.

Brittany sighed. She passed Teddy Colter's notebook back to him. Their fingers touched. She wondered if he noticed.

"That your book?" He pointed to the library book she'd taken from the back of the room. She hadn't even looked at it.

"Yes," Brittany answered. The book was missing its paper jacket—something that happened to a lot of books in the third-grade library. Her eyes skimmed the title on the spine: *Johnny Bench, King of the Reds.*

"You like Johnny Bench?" Teddy asked, wide-eyed.

"Sure." Whoever he is, she added to herself. She'd probably like him after she read his book, though. She liked stories about kings.

Teddy grinned at her as if she'd just told him he'd won a lifetime supply of baseball shirts. Grabbing his pencil, he scribbled something across the top of Brittany's notebook, then handed it back to her.

It said:

Brittany is cool!

She grinned back. Maybe being in the class with the summer birthdays wasn't so bad after all.

3

Uncles and Reptiles

Honk! Honk!

Brittany's eyes darted toward the honking car as she dashed for the bus after school.

Uncle Kevin waved at her from inside his police car. Then he opened the passenger door.

Kids boarding the bus stopped to stare, oohing and ahing.

Brittany changed course and raced toward his car.

"Look! She's getting arrested!" Sammy Varela yelled.

Brittany ignored him. She jumped into the police car. "Hi," she said to her uncle. He was her dad's younger brother.

She dumped her library book in the middle of the seat. Then she clicked the seat belt into place. "Hello, Ranger," she cooed to the German shepherd hunched in the back seat.

Ranger panted and lurched forward, trying to lick Brittany. Uncle Kevin slid open the screen of crisscrossed metal separating the front and back seats.

Uncle Kevin had told her the screen was there in case he had to give a ride to a prisoner. The thought made Brittany shiver.

He saluted, then pulled away from the curb. Brittany thought he looked handsome in his blue uniform. His blond hair was messed up, as though he'd just pulled off his hat and tossed it onto the dash.

"Your dad invited me to dinner—which means he wants me to *cook* dinner for you and Shelby."

Brittany laughed. Her mom was away on a business trip. Dad didn't like to cook. Uncle Kevin did.

"I told him I'd pick you up on the way over."

"Great." Brittany leaned forward to listen to voices and static coming over the police radio. "Can I turn on your siren?" she asked.

He raised his eyebrows at her. "You can't turn it on for fun. It would scare the daylights out of people like him." He pointed toward an elderly man strolling down the sidewalk.

Uncle Kevin had let Brittany and Corky turn on the siren one time. But it was for a special show at the airport. The siren blared for only fifteen seconds. Still, she and Corky thought it was exciting.

That was also the day they watched planes take off and land.

Brittany's heart twinged. She missed Corky.

"I didn't know you liked baseball," Uncle Kevin said.

"I do?" she asked, confused.

He tilted the library book toward her. "You like Johnny Bench?"

Popular question. "Sure, I guess so. I haven't read the book yet."

"He was one of my favorites too."

Brittany picked up the book and opened it. Inside was a picture of a man in a baseball uniform. The caption read, "Johnny Bench of the Cincinnati Reds."

Brilliant, she thought, closing the book. *That's* the reason Teddy Colter said I was cool. The *only* reason.

Uncle Kevin turned onto the Mackles' street. "Are you taking good care of my reptile friends?"

"Yep." Her uncle had named the gecko Stravinsky and the Gila monster Tchaikovsky, after his favorite Russian composers. Brittany liked the long names, but she could never get the spellings right. So she renamed them.

Now the gecko was Lizzie and the Gila monster was
Rachel. "Rachel" was one of Brittany's all-time favorite
names, even if Corky hated it. But whenever Corky
was around, Brittany called her Rachel-reptile Gilly,
so she wouldn't hurt her friend's feelings.

"I have a surprise for you when we get to my house,"
Brittany said. "Mom let me choose a new pet last weekend at the mall."

"Yeah? What'd you get? A kitten?"

"No. A turtle."

Uncle Kevin laughed. "Not another reptile!"

Brittany nodded. She liked having pets different from everyone else's.

"So what'd you name him?"

"Well," she began, riffling the pages in her library book. "I haven't come up with a good name yet, but—"

Brittany paused. The perfect name for her newest reptile popped into her mind.

Grinning at her uncle, she said, "I think I'll name him *Johnny Bench*."

4

Feisty Friends
and Silly Sisters

"**Y**ou got mail, Brit!" Shelby called. She was setting the dinner table while Uncle Kevin and Dad cooked hamburgers on the back-porch grill.

Brittany sorted through the mail on the counter until she found two envelopes with her name on them. She ripped open the first one. It was a card from her mother. On the front, a teary-eyed alligator hugged a stuffed baby alligator. Inside, it said: *I miss you. Love, Mom.*

She felt pleased her mom had chosen a card with a reptile on it. Maybe someday Mom would let her have an alligator for a pet.

Brittany set the card on the counter next to the one Shelby'd gotten from Mom. Hers had a cat on the front. Shelby wanted a cat, like everyone else. She had no imagination.

Picking up the other envelope, Brittany ripped it open. The card said:

> *You are invited to a Birthday Party*
> *for Stephanie Allen*
> *Saturday at one o'clock*
> *88 Chuckwagon Drive*
> *RSVP*

Stephanie Allen was in Ms. Hampton's class. Brittany was pleased to be invited to a party at her house, but she knew what it meant.

It meant Ms. Hampton's room would *also* have a party for Stephanie. Brittany's class would have to concentrate on math problems while sounds of singing and laughing and clapping came right through the wall.

It was hard to multiply and divide while other third-graders were having so much fun.

Brittany wondered if Corky had gotten an invitation to Stephanie's party today too. Usually they carpooled to parties with one mother or the other. Would they go together if Corky was still mad at her?

Brittany had a sudden urge to talk to her former best friend. She needed someone to sympathize with her over other kids' birthday parties.

She ran to the back porch. Dad was deep in conversation with Uncle Kevin while flipping burgers in his Barbecue Man apron.

"Can I invite Corky to dinner?" she asked, interrupting them.

He stopped talking long enough to nod at her.

Brittany dashed inside, picked up the kitchen phone, and punched in Corky's number.

"Hello?" came Corky's voice.

"Hi." Brittany wished she'd thought about what she was going to say after Corky answered.

"Is this Brit?" Her voice sounded cool.

"Um, yes. I'm calling to ask if you'd like to come over for hamburgers."

Silence.

Brittany expected Corky to say, "Did you happen to notice that I'm not speaking to you?"

"I can't," Corky said instead. "Mom already fixed meat loaf."

"That's okay," Brittany answered. "Did you get invited to Stephanie's birthday party?"

"Yeah."

Brittany sidestepped so Shelby could open the refrigerator. She felt disappointed that Corky couldn't come over. But at least they were having a conversation—sort of. "Do you want to go to the party together?"

"We'll see." Ice dripped off Corky's words.

Brittany tried again. "I'm invited to *two* birthday parties on Saturday. Stephanie's and Uncle Kevin's. My uncle's birthday is Friday, but we're having a party here Saturday night." Then she added, "Want to come?"

"We'll see."

Brittany could almost feel the frigid air billowing out of the phone receiver. She got the hint. "Well, see you tomorrow at school."

Sighing, she hung up the phone. She'd wanted to ask Corky to consider trading her glass Shetland pony for a rearing Appaloosa. Maybe now wasn't the best time to ask.

After dinner, Brittany played in the backyard with Ranger. Dad and Uncle Kevin were tossing a baseball back and forth.

Shelby sat on the steps, painting her fingernails. Brittany wished Shelby would play with her and Ranger, but her sister refused to do fun things anymore.

Shelby claimed something *horrible* might happen. Meaning her hair would get messed up. Or a fingernail might break. Or her boyfriend, Rusty, might show up and catch her acting silly.

"Heads up!" Dad shouted.

Brittany jumped to one side as the baseball bonked to the ground.

"You're supposed to catch it." He grinned at her, looking a lot like Uncle Kevin, only older.

"I didn't see it." Brittany was embarrassed at being caught off guard. Her mind was still on her phone conversation with Corky.

"Here, this might help." He jogged to the lawn chair where Brittany had tossed her mitt after she and Dad played catch yesterday. He heaved the mitt to her, then stepped close and pitched the ball underhand.

Brittany swooped the mitt in an arc, easily snagging the ball.

"Wow!" Uncle Kevin hollered from across the yard. "She's good."

"That was a baby catch," Brittany called back to him. "Watch this." She tossed the ball back to her dad, then raced toward the farthest side of the yard, Ranger at her heels.

Dad sailed the ball high, as though it were a pop fly to deep right field. Brittany ran back, then leapt into the air. She thrust out her mitt, keeping her other hand ready to cup the ball in the pocket.

The ball thwacked into the well-worn pocket. As her feet hit the ground, Brittany dropped to her left shoulder and rolled over, just for show. Coming to her knees, she held the ball in the air so the invisible umpire could see she'd caught it.

Ranger barked, dancing around her, begging for the ball.

Dad and Uncle Kevin cheered. Even Shelby joined in. All those after-dinner sessions playing catch with her dad were paying off.

Maybe she should ask Teddy Colter to play catch

sometime. She smiled to herself. Would he think that was cool too?

The sputtering sound of a motorcycle arriving in front of the house started Ranger barking again.

"Rusty's here!" Shelby called, jumping to her feet. She straightened her clothes with the palm of one hand so her nails wouldn't smudge. Crooking a knuckle, she

shoved up her red-framed glasses. Then she faced the breeze, shaking her head to style her hair while blowing on one wet nail at a time.

Brittany groaned. She tossed the ball to Uncle Kevin, then dusted the grass and leaves off her jeans. She hoped when she became a teenager, she'd still play catch and chase Ranger around the yard instead of act silly like Shelby.

5

Born Too Late

Brittany left the girls' restroom and headed back to class. Her ears caught the strain of a familiar song coming from Ms. Hampton's room:

> "*Happy birthday, dear Stephanie,*
> *Happy birthday to you.*"

Sammy Varela and Cid Quintana were in the hall. Sammy was supposed to be giving Cid her makeup spelling test. But instead the two were on tiptoe, peeking into Ms. Hampton's class, watching the party.

The old feeling of unfairness swept over Brittany. She joined the others, spying on all the fun. Soon Ms. Hampton noticed them. She pointed, frowning, toward Miss McKellips's room.

"I wish *we* could have parties," whispered Sammy, trudging back to the spelling test.

"Me too," added Cid.

"And me." Brittany tapped the hall pass against her palm, thinking. There had to be a way her class could celebrate birthdays and have parties like other classes.

She thought about the suggestion box on the windowsill. Maybe it was time someone suggested a plan for the class with the summer birthdays.

Brittany slipped into the classroom. It was silent-reading time. She hung up the hall pass and tiptoed to her seat.

As she passed Teddy Colter's desk, he mumbled something under his breath. She couldn't hear the words, but she could tell by the tone of his voice and the smirk on his face it was something mean.

Whatever Teddy whispered, Brittany bounced it back double to him.

She took her seat, thinking about birthday-party ideas for the suggestion box. She opened her notebook to scribble some notes. How could the summer-birthday class celebrate birthdays during the school year?

She remembered a story she'd once read about kids who celebrated half-birthdays six months from their real birthdays.

Brittany counted months on her fingers. It wouldn't work. Her real birthday was June 25th, so her half-birthday was December 25th. There was no school that day either.

"Brittany, this is reading time, not writing time," Miss McKellips said. She tapped her pencil on the chalkboard under the reading assignments.

Brittany felt herself blush all the way to her ears as she closed her notebook and took out her reading text.

She was in the Walrus group, so she read the assignment on the board underneath a worn picture of a red walrus.

As she flipped through the book, a page of jokes caught her eye. The funniest was: "How many seconds are there in one year? Twelve: January second, February second, March second . . ."

Brittany wondered if Corky had read the joke. She'd tell it to her later. *If* Corky would listen.

Turning to the assigned page, Brittany read a story about an author named Mary Dodge. The author was born on January 26, 1831.

"*She* wouldn't be in the baby class," Brittany mumbled. The author had written a famous book called *Hans Brinker*. It was about an ice skater in Holland.

The author's life sounded interesting. Brittany wondered if Mary Dodge celebrated birthdays at school. Then she wondered what school was like in the 1800s.

By the time the lunch bell rang, Mary Dodge's story had given Brittany a wonderful idea. As the class lined up, she tore a piece of paper from her notebook. Then she scribbled her idea on it.

Folding the paper, Brittany walked along the row of windows to the end of the line, stopping along the way to stuff the paper into the suggestion box.

The Plan

At lunch Brittany scraped every trace of coconut off her cupcake before she ate it. Then she waited for the bell. Now that Corky wasn't talking to her, she finished lunch with time left over.

Brittany heard loud voices. She peered around a row of third-graders to see what was causing the commotion at the end of the table. Corky was holding something in her hand, showing it to the kids around her.

Brittany tried to act as if she weren't curious. But she was.

Corky sat her treasure in the middle of the table. Now Brittany could see it. It was a prancing horse made out of glass. Corky must have gotten a new one for her collection.

She felt left out as she listened to her former friend

answer questions about the horse. "It's a Clydesdale," she was saying.

Brittany also felt angry. Why hadn't Corky accepted her apology—both for calling her Rachel and for telling Sammy she liked Teddy Colter?

Hadn't *she* accepted Corky's apology last summer

when Corky's family went out of town the weekend of Brittany's birthday party?

The bell rang.

Brittany carried her tray to the window in the kitchen. Teddy and Sammy were right behind her.

She sat her tray down with a clatter, then turned.

"Hi," Teddy said.

"Hi." Brittany waited, watching him in his Philadelphia Phillies T-shirt. Was he going to talk to her? In front of Sammy Varela?

"What's that?" Teddy asked, pointing toward the ceiling.

"What's what?" Brittany looked up.

Teddy flung a Nerf ball at her.

Startled, Brittany flinched, thrusting out her hands to catch it. The ball fumbled through her fingers and flumped to the floor.

"You catch like a girl!" Teddy cried, snatching up the ball. He raced away laughing with Sammy.

Brittany's face burned. She was *good* at catching balls. He'd tricked her! That was the only reason she'd dropped it.

She stormed out of the cafeteria, glaring at anyone who looked as if they were about to ask why her face was red.

How could she ever have liked Teddy Colter? He was a jerk.

In class Brittany finished her math early. She offered to straighten the art cabinet. Miss McKellips awarded her a good-citizen mark.

For the rest of the afternoon, Brittany stayed at her desk, a model student, following all the rules. It earned her another mark.

And for the rest of the afternoon, Sammy and Teddy teased her about dropping the Nerf ball. "Klutz, klutz, klutz," they singsonged. Only they did it when the teacher wasn't listening.

Teddy even passed around a note that said:

Brittany is a klutz!

How could she go from cool to klutz so fast?

By the end of the day Brittany had a headache from all the teasing. She wanted to go to the nurse. But it was time for Miss McKellips to open the suggestion box.

Today there were three suggestions. The teacher perched on the edge of her desk and unfolded the first one. "Cid Quintana suggests that we be allowed to get drinks anytime we need to."

"I'm thirsty all the time," Cid explained, clutching her throat.

"Yeah, but what if someone went to the water fountain ninety times in one day?" asked Sammy Varela.

The class mumbled their agreement.

"Do we need to define some rules?" Miss McKellips asked.

Brittany glanced at Corky. It always made them laugh when Miss McKellips used her favorite phrase: "define some rules."

Corky was grinning—but at her desk, not at Brittany.

"How about two trips in the morning and two in the afternoon?" Cid replied. "On your honor."

"Vote by raising your hand if you agree with Cid," Miss McKellips said.

Everyone raised a hand except Teddy Colter. He raised two.

Brittany refused to laugh at him like everyone else.

"Settled." The teacher unfolded the next suggestion. She paused to read it. "I'm sorry, Teddy, but I don't think making girls stay off the softball field during recess is a fair suggestion."

The girls booed.

Teddy pounded a fist on his desk. His suggestion had been vetoed without a vote.

Miss McKellips unfolded the last note. Brittany's heart skittered.

"Brittany Mackle suggests that we each choose a person from history who does *not* have a summer birthday, then adopt his or her birthday for our own."

The room was quiet. Sammy's hand shot up. "Does that mean we can have birthday parties like other classes?"

"I assume that's what Brittany has in mind."

Brittany nodded.

The class cheered.

Her heart skittered faster. The class liked her suggestion!

"Sounds as if we don't need to vote," the teacher said.

"Great idea, Brit," Cid whispered.

"However," Miss McKellips continued, "we need to define some rules."

Brittany giggled. This time Corky smiled at her.

The teacher stood, tapping Brittany's suggestion against one cheek. "Your homework for tonight is to choose the person from history you want to be. Write

down his or her name and birth date. Then turn it in to me in the morning."

"What if two people pick the same person?" Teddy asked.

"Good question, Ted. Let's ask Brittany, since it's her suggestion."

All eyes turned to Brittany. She sat up straight in her chair, willing her face not to turn red. "Um, how about . . . first come, first served? That way we won't have twenty-six George Washingtons."

The class laughed. Brittany felt pleased with her answer. Her face didn't feel flushed at all.

"Miss McKellips?" Cid asked. "Do girls have to pick only women from history and boys only men?"

"Brittany?" the teacher said, passing the question to her.

"No." She remembered how everyone had teased Corky when she cut her hair. Maybe if girls could be boy characters—and boys could be girls—kids would stop calling her Corky Boy.

"Can we bring treats from home on our new birthdays?" Corky asked.

"Of course," Miss McKellips said. "We'll have regular birthday parties, just like other classes."

Everyone whooped and applauded.

"Except for one thing."

Brittany's heart stalled. She was enjoying the smiles and thumbs-up signs coming from kids around her. But from the look on the teacher's face, she knew there was going to be more to it than parties and treats and singing songs.

"On your borrowed birthday, you will turn in a report on the life of the person you've chosen. Then, before your party, you will give the class a short presentation."

The room became as quiet as silent-reading time. Except for a few moans and groans.

"Thanks a lot, Brittany," echoed in her ears.

"Way to go, klutz," whispered Teddy.

"Terrific," she mumbled, slumping at her desk. "I just gave the class a homework assignment. . . ."

7

The Girl with All the Answers

That night after dinner, Brittany sprinkled gecko food into Lizzie's bowl. Then she put Gilamonster food into Rachel's cage.

Brittany picked up her newest pet, Johnny Bench. She let him lumber across her dresser to the pile of turtle food she'd sprinkled in one corner.

He twisted his skinny green neck to gaze at her. It looked as if he were asking why he had to hike so far for his dinner. Feeling guilty, Brittany picked him up by his shell and moved him closer to the food.

She was growing so attached to her three scaly pets, she'd started bringing home library books about reptiles. Maybe she'd be an expert someday. Brittany Mackle, Reptologist.

After Johnny Bench ate, Brittany put him back into

his dish. Then she sprawled across her bed to read about Mary Dodge. She was the person from history Brittany had picked for the Birthday Project—as it was now being called.

Shelby had taken her to the library before dinner to check out the book *Hans Brinker* and to find information about the author.

Brittany had plenty of time to plan her talk, since Mary Dodge's birthday was four months away. Still, she was eager to read the skating book.

"Brit!" came her dad's voice. "Telephone. Again."

She sighed, heading for the phone in the hall. It had

been ringing all evening. No one in class seemed able to pick a character from history without advice from her.

She felt as if she were Miss McKellips, "defining the rules" for her own suggestion.

First it was Cid Quintana calling to ask if the person had to be dead.

No, Brittany had told her.

Then Sammy Varela called to ask if he could pick Uncle Sam, because he already had an Uncle Sam costume from last Halloween.

Brittany explained that Uncle Sam had been born on the fourth of July. What was the point of choosing someone with a summer birthday? Uncle Sam would've been in the baby class too.

Then Teddy Colter called. Last week a call from Teddy Colter would have been more exciting than a day at Disneyland. But she was so angry with him for tormenting her this week, she was almost sorry to hear his voice on the other end of the line.

He wanted her to promise that he could be George Washington. It wasn't fair, because Teddy had given a report on Washington last year. All he had to do was give the same report. Brittany reminded him about the rule of first come, first served. She couldn't promise him anything.

This time the call was from Corky.

"Hi," Brittany said. Was Corky ready to be friends again?

"I have an important question." Corky sounded mysterious. "I want to borrow one of your relatives for my birthday character."

"What?"

"Can it be a person who's still living?"

"Yeah."

"Does it have to be a famous person?"

"Well, no. I guess not."

"I want to be your uncle Kevin."

"What! Why?"

"Didn't you tell me his birthday is Friday?"

Brittany glanced at her calendar. The day after tomorrow was circled in red and marked "Unc. K.'s B'day."

"Yes."

"Good. I get my report over with right away instead of worrying about it for months. We get out of math on Friday afternoon for my party. And if I interview your uncle about his life, maybe he'll let me wear his police hat to school. And bring Ranger. And—"

"Wait." Brittany felt strange about Corky borrowing her own uncle's life. She almost felt jealous. "Your birthday character has to be someone from history."

Corky was quiet for a moment. "Isn't history anything that happened in the past?"

"Yeah."

"Well, your uncle was born in the past, wasn't he? And he became a police officer in the past."

Brittany had to agree. "But," she said, stalling, "are you sure you want to be a—you know—*boy* character?" Wasn't Corky worried that it might lead to more teasing?

"Yes."

Brittany hadn't heard such determination in Corky's voice since she'd joined Little League last spring. But Corky had a habit of closing her eyes whenever she batted or fielded, so she'd spent a lot of time on the bench—to the relief of a lot of the boys.

Still, she'd tried.

"You know," Corky added, "*girls* can be police officers too. And that's what I want to be when I grow up."

Brittany hesitated.

"I'll trade you my new Clydesdale for your Palomino pony," Corky said.

They'd traded and retraded glass horses a zillion times. Brittany didn't even remember which horses belonged to her.

"Well?" Corky urged her to make a decision.

Brittany still felt unsure. Yet she'd love to own Corky's Clydesdale. It was the biggest glass horse she'd ever seen. "Okay," she said with a sigh. "I'll call Uncle Kevin and ask him to give us a ride home tomorrow so you can interview him."

"Great," Corky said. "Sit with me on the bus in the morning?"

"Sure."

"Oh, and Brit? Knock, knock."

Brittany chuckled. Her old friend was back to normal. "Who's there?"

"Police."

"Police who?"

"Police don't forget to call your uncle Kevin."

Brittany groaned and hung up the phone.

Shelby came down the hall. Hot rollers jiggled with every move. A beauty mask was smeared blue across her face. And her glasses sat cockeyed because of the rollers on the sides of her head.

Shelby grinned. "How'd you like to be *me* for a character? My birthday is next month. You can wear my pompom uniform and tell your class all about my life. And—"

Brittany plugged her ears. Shelby was the *last* character on earth she wanted to be.

Insulted, Shelby stuck her blue nose in the air and hurried down the hall.

Brittany returned to her bedroom. She flopped onto the bed, pulling a pillow over her head, and wished Mom were home this week. Her mother's hugs and advice would be welcome tonight.

Why was everyone taking such an interest in this little suggestion of hers? It was starting to get out of hand.

8

Win a Few, Lose a Few

The next morning Brittany's classmates rushed to turn in the names of their birthday characters. Miss McKellips clipped the papers together in the order received—keeping Brittany's rule of first come, first served. All were due by recess.

During seatwork the teacher wrote "Birthday Project" on the board, then listed the names of people already chosen so the class could see whose birthdays they'd be celebrating.

The list included presidents, movie stars, authors, athletes, astronauts, rock stars, politicians—and Brittany's uncle.

Brittany hadn't turned in her paper yet. She felt sure no one else had chosen Mary Dodge.

A note plopped onto her reading book. It was from Teddy Colter.

Dear Brit,

Help! Sammy picked George Washington first! I can't think of another birthday character. Do you have any suggestions? Hurry!

Your friend, Ted

Now Teddy was her *friend*? After being mean to her all week?

Brittany sighed. Everyone in class was trying to be her friend all of a sudden.

She leaned back in her chair to think. Even though she was angry with Teddy, she would help him. After all, the Birthday Project *was* her idea, and she wanted it to be a success.

She scratched her head. Who could Teddy be?

Brittany remembered the sentences he'd written about baseball. Of course. Choosing someone for Teddy was easy.

Opening her desk, Brittany peeked at the book about Johnny Bench. A page in front listed information about his batting average and stuff like that. It also mentioned his birthday.

Keeping one eye on the teacher, Brittany flipped through the book. She didn't want to lose a good-citizen mark for not doing her reading. All she needed was one more mark to make ten. And a bingo.

When Miss McKellips turned away, Brittany ducked her head inside the desk and quickly scanned the page. "Birth date," it read, "December 7."

She closed her desk and ripped a fresh sheet of paper from her notebook. Then she wrote:

> *Person from history: Johnny Bench*
> *Birthday: December 7*

It was almost time for recess. Brittany glanced at Teddy. He sat there in his Oakland A's T-shirt, gaping at her as though he were up to bat with two out and the bases loaded.

She started to hand him the paper. As he reached for it, all the things he'd done this week whirled through her mind: snapping at her, making her drop the Nerf ball, laughing at her with Sammy, calling her a klutz. Then she thought about his suggestion to keep all the girls off the softball field.

A crazy idea popped into Brittany's head. Snatching the paper back, she scribbled her own name at the top. Then she fished inside her desk for another piece of paper. It read:

Person from history: Mary Dodge
Birthday: January 26

She erased her name and wrote "Teddy Colter," then handed the paper to him just as the recess bell rang.

Teddy's face got all scrunchy. "A lady?" he gasped. "You want me to be a *lady*?"

Miss McKellips walked down the aisle, collecting the rest of the papers. She took Brittany's, then pried Teddy's from his fingers.

"Mary Dodge is an author." Brittany pulled the book

Hans Brinker from her desk and handed it to Teddy. "Here, you can read her book."

"But I like sports stories."

"It *is* a sports story, see?" Brittany pointed to the boy skating on the cover.

"Is he playing hockey?"

"No. He's ice skating."

"Ice skating isn't a sport!" Teddy studied the picture, looking interested in spite of his protest.

"Kids! Outside," Miss McKellips ordered.

Brittany wasn't about to lose a good-citizen mark. She scuttled out the door.

Toward the end of recess, a first-grader took a dive knees first off the monkey bars. In spite of the little boy's howling, Brittany helped him to the nurse and stayed with him while his knees were cleaned and bandaged.

Brittany hadn't helped the first-grader with a reward in mind. Still, it netted her good-citizen mark number ten. Bingo.

Miss McKellips let her look at the good-citizen list in the afternoon and choose what she wanted to do. A few items tempted her: extra recess, a whole afternoon in the library, office helper. But Brittany had already made up her mind. Sitting next to Teddy Colter had changed her feelings about liking him. She wanted Corky to have the same experience, so she'd never get angry with Brittany over Teddy again.

"Well?" Miss McKellips asked.

"I want to change desks with Corky."

"You mean—change desks so you can *sit* next to Corky?"

"No. I want Corky to sit where I sit now."

"Okay." Miss McKellips looked at her as if she thought Brittany had lost her good sense. "As long as it's okay with Corky."

It was okay with Corky. As a matter of fact, she was beside herself. First, because her desk was now next to Teddy Colter's. And second, because she got to ride in Uncle Kevin's police car again.

After school Corky jumped into the front seat as soon as the police car stopped. Brittany climbed into the back and sat next to Ranger, scratching him behind the ears.

As Uncle Kevin pulled into the street, Corky opened her notebook and began asking him a list of questions, jotting answers as she went.

Brittany thought some of the questions and answers were silly, but she didn't say anything:

> Why do police officers wear blue uniforms?
> (To match their blue police socks.)
> What's your middle name?
> (Barry.)
> Why aren't you married?
> (Too young—ha ha ha.)

Uncle Kevin and Corky stayed at the Mackles' house for dinner so she could learn all about being a police officer. Then Uncle Kevin called Miss McKellips and made plans to visit her class the next afternoon. He even promised to bring Ranger and let each student sit in his police car.

Brittany wished *she'd* thought of using her uncle as a birthday character instead of some dead author, or a baseball player she'd never heard of.

Wandering into the backyard, she played with Ranger for a while. Then she went to her room, fed the reptiles, and rearranged her glass horses.

Sounds of laughter drifted to her room. She closed the bedroom door so she didn't have to listen.

When Mrs. Salerno arrived to pick up Corky, Brit-

tany didn't feel like saying good night. Dad made her come out to the living room anyway.

Corky was pulling on her jacket, still chattering away to Uncle Kevin. Dad started talking to Mrs. Salerno. No one paid any attention to Brittany at all.

She moved close to her uncle, slipping her hand into his. He stopped talking to Corky and smiled at his niece, squeezing her hand.

Together they said good night to Corky and Mrs. Salerno. It made Brittany feel a whole lot better.

9

Friends Again

Mrs. Salerno drove the girls to school in the morning so they didn't have to carry Corky's birthday treats on the bus.

Brittany peeked inside the foil-covered bowl on her lap. Mrs. Salerno had baked multi-colored cookies shaped like policemen's badges, dogs, pistols, and hats.

"Here," Corky said, twisting around in the front seat. "I almost forgot." She held out her glass Clydesdale.

Brittany took the horse. She fished in her pocket for the Palomino pony and handed it to Corky.

Brittany was excited about the coming day. She felt proud that her suggestion had turned out so well. Now the class with the summer birthdays would have parties all year long. It was even better than the other classes. They each had parties for only half the year.

When they arrived at school, the girls got permission

to deliver the party treats to Miss McKellips's classroom before the bell rang. Then they headed toward the exit at the end of the hall.

Brittany opened the double doors and stepped onto the playground.

"Look out!" someone shouted.

She whipped around. A Nerf ball was spiraling straight at Corky's head.

This time Brittany was ready. She leapt into the air,

caught the ball in one hand, landed on her left foot, twirled in a circle, then spiked the ball onto the concrete the way her dad had taught her.

She held her hands high in a victory sign, like the football players on television. A few kids around her cheered. Teddy Colter and Sammy Varela gaped in awe.

Snatching the ball off the ground, Brittany hurled it back to Teddy, giving it her wrist-twist as she let go. "Here's one for you!" she called. The ball headed straight toward him, then curved away.

He grabbed for it and missed. Behind him, a second-grade girl caught it. Everyone laughed.

Brittany smirked at him. "You catch like a little boy," she said.

Sammy Varela laughed so hard, his face turned to-mato red.

Teddy didn't laugh at all. He yanked his ball away from the second-grader's clasp and stormed toward the outfield.

Brittany felt sure he'd never call her "klutz" again.

• • •

The day seemed too long. It was hard, waiting for the middle of the afternoon, when Miss McKellips would say, "Clear off your desks and get ready for our first class birthday party."

In the morning Corky was in such a giggly mood, she lost three good-citizen marks before quieting down. Brittany thought Corky's good mood was more from sitting next to Teddy Colter than having a birthday party in her honor.

The episode on the playground before school had only convinced Corky that Teddy liked her, or he wouldn't have thrown his Nerf ball at her head. She had a lot to learn, Brittany thought.

By lunch Corky's sunny day had turned cloudy. She stormed to the cafeteria ahead of everyone else.

"What's wrong?" Brittany asked, catching up with her.

"Teddy and Sammy, *that's* what's wrong."

"What did they do?" Brittany was secretly pleased the two were bugging Corky now instead of her. "Are they calling you Corky Boy?"

"No. They're calling me Police Boy."

Brittany held her breath to keep from laughing. Corky was learning already.

"Why did I have to pick a *boy* character? Now Teddy will *never* like me."

"Guess what?" Brittany said, grabbing a tray and silverware.

"What?"

"I picked a boy character too."

"You did?" Corky almost smiled. "Who?"

"Johnny Bench. And one of the other girls picked Alan Shepard, the first American in space. And—last I heard—Cid was trying to decide between Elvis Presley and Martin Luther King."

"No kidding?" Corky looked relieved. "Did any of the boys pick girls for the Birthday Project?"

"I know one did."

"Who?"

"Teddy Colter." Brittany filled her in on the name switch. "Next time he calls you Police Boy, just call him Mary Dodge."

"Thank you, thank you, thank you!" Corky gushed. "You're the best friend I ever had!"

She zipped right back to her giggly mood and lost two more good-citizen marks before party time.

· · · · · · · · · · 10 · · · · · · · · ·

The Birthday Party

"**P**lease clear off your desks and get ready for our first class birthday party," Miss McKellips said, winking at Brittany.

Brittany felt tingly, as though the balloons bobbing around the room were filled with excitement instead of air.

Uncle Kevin sat in a third-grade chair at the back of the room. He looked uncomfortable. It reminded Brittany of Goldilocks in "The Three Bears," sitting in the chair that was *much too small* and breaking it.

Next to Uncle Kevin lay Ranger, ears alert, panting. Police dogs were well trained. Brittany knew Ranger would obey Uncle Kevin's instructions and behave. Still, all the third-graders were turned in their seats, watching the dog.

"Eyes front," Miss McKellips said. She leaned against a table arranged with police cookies, cupcakes, and punch. "Corky has picked games to play, songs to sing, and prizes to give away. But first, she will give a report on her birthday character."

The class applauded as Corky marched to the front of the room. She wore a dark-blue skirt with matching socks and a light-blue blouse. Over that she wore Uncle Kevin's jacket, with each sleeve rolled up six times.

On her head Uncle Kevin's hat was tipped at an angle to keep it from falling over her eyes.

Corky unfolded her report. "My birthday character from history is Kevin Barry Mackle, police officer. Officer Mackle was born—"

Corky glanced at the audience and froze. Her hands began to tremble. From two seats back, Brittany heard the paper rustling.

The room became so quiet, the quiet sounded loud.

"September thirtieth," Brittany whispered, trying to cue her friend.

"Sep . . . Sep . . . Sep," said Corky.

Brittany's heart pounded. Her friend was dying up there. Out of all the third-graders, Corky was the last person Brittany expected to get stage fright.

From the back of the room Ranger gave a soft whimper. He seemed to know someone needed saving, and that was what he'd been bred and raised to do—save people. Only this time there wasn't a thing Ranger could do.

Teddy and Sammy snickered, mumbling together about Corky.

"I bounce it back double to you," Brittany hissed under her breath.

She jumped to her feet and was next to Corky in two seconds. "Today is September thirtieth," she said loud and clear. "Officer Mackle's birthday."

Corky snapped her head around to stare at Brittany. The police hat fell over her eyes.

Brittany snatched the hat off Corky's head and held it high so the class could see it better. "Corky asked me to help," she said. "I'll hold the hat while she tells you about it."

Corky's lips quivered.

Brittany thought it might be a nervous smile.

Corky took a deep breath and focused on the paper in front of her. "A police officer's hat carries the state symbol on the front." Her voice sounded shaky. "It's called a hat badge."

Brittany pointed at the hat badge as though she were a model on television. She kept waiting for her face to heat up and turn red, but it didn't. Well, maybe a little. But she knew her face couldn't possibly be as red as Corky's face right now.

"Thank you, Brit," Corky said in a much stronger voice. "Mr. Mackle decided to become a police officer at the age of twelve, when he was injured in a bike accident. A kind police officer drove him home, then to a doctor."

Brittany edged toward her desk. Corky seemed fine now.

"Next, Brittany will hold up a pair of handcuffs," Corky said.

Brittany followed Corky's instructions. She set Uncle Kevin's hat on the table and picked up a pair of handcuffs. Then she walked around the room while Corky talked about them.

"Now I'd like to introduce my birthday character, Officer Mackle."

The class applauded as Uncle Kevin stepped to the front of the room, Ranger prancing at his heels.

Corky grabbed Brittany's arm. "Thanks for saving me," she whispered.

Brittany grinned, hurrying to her desk.

"Officer Mackle will show you how he works with his trained dog," Corky explained. "After we eat, we'll go outside to his police car."

Again the room fell quiet. Brittany was proud,

watching her uncle. But she wondered why his face had turned as white as Miss McKellips's chalk. And she wondered why all he'd said so far was "Uh, uh, uh."

He shuffled his feet, bent to pat Ranger's head, then stood tall. "Uh," he began again. "This is my dog, uh, uh—"

"Ranger," Brittany whispered, her stomach tensing into a knot. Was Uncle Kevin going to die up there as badly as Corky had?

"Uh, uh, uh," he said.

Brittany groaned, then rushed to the front of the room again.

Both Uncle Kevin and Ranger looked happy to see her.

"This is Ranger," she said, moving across the room. "Ranger, come!"

Ranger bounded toward her.

"Sit," she commanded.

Ranger sat.

"Now Uncle Kev—I mean, Officer Mackle—will show you how Ranger is trained to do what he's told."

"Thank you, Brit," her uncle said, recovering full use of the English language. "Ranger, here!" He tapped his leg and Ranger bounded to his side. Then Uncle Kevin explained how police dogs are trained.

Corky and Brittany giggled at each other.

Uncle Kevin was fine now. Brittany could tell he'd won a few fans by the expressions on Teddy and Sammy's faces. Especially after he handcuffed them together.

Brittany tiptoed to her desk. Her own speech would be a piece of cake after all this.

But, a voice inside her head argued, what if every third-grader in the room gets stagefright? What if I have

to jump up and help Teddy talk about Mary Dodge?
And Cid talk about Elvis? Or Martin Luther King?

And—?

And worse.

What if Miss McKellips calls off the Birthday Project
because none of the third-graders can give speeches?

Brittany stared at the long list of characters from
history on the chalkboard. Maybe she'd better study
the lives of all those people—just in case.

Her brilliant suggestion was turning into an awful lot
of work.

She sighed. Well, first things first. She'd start with the life of Johnny Bench. Maybe she should write to him. Maybe he'd send her a Cincinnati Reds shirt. Wouldn't Teddy Colter die of envy?

But she had lots of time to plan her own talk. First, she fully intended to enjoy the class with the summer birthdays' first official party.

Right here, right now.

Sitting up straight, Brittany joined in the singing:

> *"Happy birthday, Corky and Officer Mackle,*
> *Happy birthday to you!"*